# The Amazing Time Travelling Adventures of Professor McGinty in Ancient Greece

**by**

**E.R.Reilly and Richard Allen**

PUBLISHED IN GREAT BRITAIN BY
SANTIAGO PRESS
PO BOX 8808
BIRMINGHAM
B30 2LR

Email for orders and enquiries:
santiago@reilly19.freeserve.co.uk

ISBN 0-9539229-7-9

Printed and bound in India by
OM Authentic Media, P.O. Box 2190, Secunderabad 500 003
E-mail: printing@ombooks.org

Hello, hello, hello, you wonderful person, and congratulations on choosing to read all about me! I am, of course, the world's only time travelling detective, Professor McGinty! It shows great taste (and a certain amount of madness!) in wanting to read all about my exciting adventures into the distant past, to times of wonder and to places of mystery. I have travelled far and wide, through time and space, to find out about the fascinating lives of people that lived in the past, and to bring a little something back to add to my museum of incredible stuff!

First of all, let me tell you a little bit more about myself and my modest home. I live in an old stately house, forgotten by the rest of the world, kept hidden by the creeping plants that wind their way up the walls to the tops of the turrets. I spend most of my time in the East Wing, in my special secret room; a room that only I have the key to. This is where I house my wondrous museum of truly amazing things. Here, I keep the items and artefacts ("stuff"!) that I have collected from all over the world and from all over time so that I can reminisce about my spectacular adventures. The dusty shelves are laden with weird and wonderful objects. Ahhh! What stories they can tell! I also keep a selection of my beloved books in this room. There are probably a thousand leather-bound journals in there and I have read every single one! It is in here that I spend most of my spare time, relaxing after my hectic time-travelling detective work, reading a well-thumbed dog-eared book, sitting in front of a roaring open fire and listening to the gentle tick-tocking of my majestic grandfather clock.

Even though it has a thousand books in it, I don't call that room the Library. No. My Library is in the West Wing of the house and it has ten thousand books in it! You may have guessed by now that I love to read - well, I am a Professor, you know! You don't get to be a Professor by watching telly all the time!

It's a very hard job to keep my house clean, although I do have the Johnson brothers, who polish my lovely chandeliers for me, and I also have Mrs Broome. No, don't laugh! That is her name! Mrs Broome is my housekeeper, and she spends many an hour cleaning and polishing all the ancient relics that I have collected over the years.

She also cooks my tea for me every night.

Travelling through time, I have eaten many splendid foods you can only dream of! I have dined on flamingos' tongues with the Romans and feasted on hyena with the Ancient Egyptians, but when I return home, my favourite food of all has to be baked beans on toast. Nothing beats it! Yum, yum!

The only other person that comes to my house is Mr Pegg, the postman. I often help him out when he has trouble delivering the post, but that is another story.

Now it is time to tell you all about my partner in time travel and detection, the remarkable Doctor Hoot. Doctor Hoot is, in fact, an owl. An extremely large owl! In fact, so large that he is nearly six feet tall! (And that is very large for an owl.) Doctor Hoot has been my companion for many, many years. Without him, my adventures would not have been half so much fun (or, indeed, as dangerous!). Doctor Hoot and I are from no particular time, but we do spend quite a lot of time living in the present day. One reason for this is that Doctor Hoot loves to watch Eastenders!

Throughout my travels, I have become a well known wanderer about town in Tudor times (ugh, stinky!), a most famous fellow amongst Viking raiders, and, not to mention, an exceptional embalmer in Ancient Egypt.

But this story I am about to tell you is all about my travels to the golden age of Ancient Greece. This adventure started when Doctor Hoot was sitting in front of the television one day. We had just finished eating our favourite dinner, beans on toast.

On the day of our adventure in time travel to Ancient Greece, Doctor Hoot was sitting there in front of the television and he'd managed to intercept the remote control before I could. He was busy flicking through the TV channels. Well, don't you just hate it when someone else gets hold of the remote control before you do? It drives me mad. He'd been flicking through the channels for about three hours, and, as you can imagine, I was getting a little bit fed up. Three or four hours of channel flicking was really making me quite mad. I needed to do something about it.

I decided to take the Doctor to somewhere where we could get some real culture. Well, where they invented it, in Ancient Greece. We were going to go to an Ancient Greek theatre and see a real Ancient Greek play.

"But I will miss Eastenders," complained the Doctor.

I told you he is a huge fan of Eastenders. I can't stand it. He loves that, and football! I think it's Birmingham United or something he supports.

Anyway, I wanted to take him somewhere immediately to get away from the TV and to give him some culture. So, I grabbed hold of him and strapped him into

the Time Machine next to me, and I set the coordinates for Ancient Greece, 429 BC. I pressed the start button.

The machine began to shake. The machine began to whirr and the whole room began to fill with smoke.

I know some of you may think this is quite an alarming thing to happen, but, trust me, this happens every time I press the start button on the Time Machine.

When the smoke began to clear, our surroundings had changed. We'd arrived in the middle of a magnificent Ancient Greek temple, called the Parthenon, surrounded by pillars with a huge golden statue in the centre.

"Where are we?" said the Doctor.

"Ancient Greece," I said.

"Uhh, I don't suppose they've got any

TVs then?"

"No, I'm afraid not," I said. "They haven't invented it yet. We are here to get some proper culture at the theatre."

"Oh, all right then," said the Doctor.

He really, really didn't like travelling in time too much. I can tell when he's being a bit grumpy because his head twitches from side to side rather too quickly for my liking. I know why he gets so nervous.

He keeps thinking that we are going to be trapped in the past. I do understand his concerns because, whenever anybody sees the Time Machine, they always take it home. I don't blame them really because who wouldn't take a Time Machine home if they found one? You would, wouldn't you? Yes, of course you would. You are a most intelligent human being. You must be, or you wouldn't have the good sense to read this brilliant book. If I was standing next to you, I would give you a big hug!

I always want to get home and, of course, I get a bit frightened at the thought of being stuck in the past, but the ability to travel through time is so exciting, I would risk anything to be able to keep visiting the past. You would have to decide for yourself if you would risk travelling to the past.  If anybody ever asks you to try out their Time Machine, remember that, if you get stuck in the past, you may never see your family and friends again.  But I am very brave indeed and so I told Doctor Hoot to show a stiff upper beak and we set off to have a bit of a look around.

The temple was magnificent.  It was a bit like a church built for one of the Ancient Greek Gods.  They had loads of them.  This particular temple, the Parthenon, was built for the Goddess Athena, who was the Goddess of Wisdom, War and the Olive Tree!

Well, we set off down the steps into the town, looking behind us at just how magnificent this temple looked.  But, coming up the steps towards us, we saw about three hundred angry looking Greeks.

They were probably wondering what all the smoke was doing coming out of their brand new temple, and wanted to get us for it. We thought that we had better get out of there as quickly as possible. So we both ran back up the steps to the Time Machine, strapped ourselves in, set the coordinates for home and I pressed the start button. But nothing happened!

Now, that wasn't a normal thing to happen when I pressed the start button. For some reason, the Time Machine had broken and, by now, these Ancient Greek people were gathering round us and starting to mumble things like, "We worship you, oh, Goddess Athena."

"Eh?" I said.

"They think you're the Goddess Athena," said Doctor Hoot.

"Me, a Goddess?" I said. "But I'm a bloke."

"Yes, but in Ancient Greece, they believed all sorts of things were Gods. One day a tree appeared to a man and they thought that it was the God, Zeus," said the Doctor.

"Oh, well, appearing in these weird clothes with all this smoke in my Time Machine, is going to make them think that I am a God."

I kept protesting to them, "I'm not a God, I am not a God."

But they just kept shouting back, "Athena, Athena."

These people were a bit bonkers if they thought that I was the Goddess Athena! Today people would think that anybody saying that a tree was a God would be stark raving bonkers. People would probably call for some men to come in a large van and carry you off in a strait jacket. If you were to tell your friends that you found a shark in your custard they would probably think that you were telling a fib. But, believe it or not, they really used to believe that Gods appeared to people as all kinds of strange things. Now, I strongly advise you to believe it, because I am one of very few people who is lucky enough to be a time traveller and I can tell you from my own travels to Ancient Greece that it is completely true.

They picked us up in the Time Machine and dragged us off to a man called Pericles. Now Pericles, I suppose, was a bit like our Prime Minister. He was sort of the Prime Minister of Ancient Greece and he pretty

much invented the way that we run our country nowadays. You know, the way that somebody thinks of something and everyone gets to vote as to whether they like it or they don't.

In fact, you may be interested to know that we get the word "democracy" from the Ancient Greeks. Not everybody was allowed to vote in Ancient Greece. The people who were not allowed to vote were the poor people, slaves, women and people under the age of thirty. So really, the only people that voted were rich men over the age of thirty.

Well, Pericles pretty much changed that and invented democracy. But as a person, he was quite rude to other people and famous for being really rude to certain people. I thought he would see straight away that I wasn't the Goddess Athena. But I am afraid he was as daft as the others. He was there shouting, "Athena, Athena."

"I am not Athena," I kept yelling.

But he didn't believe me. He took the Time Machine from us and hid it somewhere we were never going to find it. We were trapped in Ancient Greece. I was very frightened indeed. Imagine how frightening it is to be in another time and another place only to find that someone has stolen your Time Machine. I could tell that poor Doctor Hoot was even more frightened than I was. I decided to keep the Doctor as busy as I could so that he didn't dwell too long on our predicament. The only thing that made me feel safe was the feeling that we were being treated like guests of honour.

So we decided to have a bit of a look around. I knew that I had to try and find where Pericles had hidden the Time Machine. The streets were quite narrow and shaded and the houses looked weird.

Most of the houses had red tiled roofs and white walls, and the streets were cobbled. I could see very easily which of the people were rich and which were poor. The poor people all had tanned skin. It was obvious that the rich people liked to keep their skin pale because they had servants carrying umbrellas over them to keep them in the shade.

All the houses had small windows. I wondered why. But when I stepped inside one of the houses, I could see why straight away. It was so cool inside. Nowadays our houses have got huge windows. So in the summer we tend to sit there getting cooked. But, in Ancient Greece, they weren't daft, they built small windows in their houses so at least they could have somewhere to go where it was nice and cool. Just because people lived before television had been invented doesn't mean that were any less intelligent than people who watch Eastenders.

So you might be wondering why they were silly enough to believe that Gods appeared as trees and yet clever enough to build homes that kept them cool in warm weather. Even today, people believe in things that may seem strange to others. Since I have been travelling to other times, I've learned to respect other people's points of view. I wonder what people from

Ancient Greece would say if they were to travel to the twenty first century. Maybe they would think that we are all a bit odd for watching Eastenders.

Inside the house, it was a bit dark. A bit too dark. I kept bumping into the furniture. Pericles lit something called an oil lamp. It was a weird little thing. It looked like a shoe but made out of clay. They filled it with oil and lit it. Not only did it light up the room, it also filled up the room with stinky smoke. I could hardly breathe. That was the way that they would light up their houses at night in those days.

I suppose that's why the streets were so tiny as well. To try and keep cool because the shade gives people a cool place to sleep. But all of these streets led down to a huge marketplace in the centre of town called the Agora. The Doctor and I had a well earned sleep and then, in the morning, we set out to see the Agora for ourselves.

Agora sounds good. Agora is a Greek word. It doesn't mean shops or Tesco or markets, it actually means big open space.

And that's what it was. A huge, open space filled with all sorts of stalls and market shops. This is where they sell all sorts of things. There was a shoe shop, a weapon shop, someone selling chickens, someone selling fish and grain. It was a busy place with lots of people talking at the same time. There was quite a strong smell of animals and fish. It was a pleasant smell though.

There was also a shop selling people. Yes, not to eat, though! No, they were selling slaves. But at least in Ancient Greece they were reasonably nice to their slaves. Yes, the Romans were horrible to their slaves. They made them sleep with the animals. But in Ancient Greece they believed that if you looked after your slave, hopefully he or she would look after you. The idea that any person should actually own another person seems completely awful to us today but in 429 BC it was very normal indeed.

I didn't want to buy a slave. I thought about popping into the shoe shop though. That looked strange to me. The shoe shop hadn't got any shoes in it. No, there was just a man in there standing on a table.

What happened was, you walked into the shoe shop, said, "Hello. Can I have a pair of sandals please?"

And the shopkeeper would say, "Certainly, jump on the table."

Eh?

Well, you would jump on the table and you would also stand on a thick piece of leather. That's cow skin, uggghhh! Make sure you take it off the cow first! Then the shopkeeper would get an incredibly

sharp knife and chop around the shape of your feet, so he could make a pair of sandals exactly right for your feet. So rather than buying a pair of shoes that would fit just anyone, you bought a pair of sandals made especially for you. Umm.

They had all sorts of other shops. There was a potter's shop, and the man in there was making pots and toys. There was another shop where a man was selling animals. There was an armoury shop selling

weapons and swords and shields. I thought I would pop in there and maybe try on a helmet.

At the armoury, I tried on this magnificent helmet. It was pretty heavy because it was made of bronze. Other than a helmet, they didn't wear much armour at all. A helmet, if you could afford it, some breast plate to cover up the front of your body, and, if you were really lucky, some things Doctor Hoot thought were a bit like shin pads. They were called Greaves.

Well, Pericles noticed I had taken a great interest in the armour and suggested that we pop down to the docks to have a look at one of their war ships. Ooh, I thought we might as well make the best of being trapped in Ancient Greece, so off we trotted, following Pericles, all the way

down to the docks. I left Doctor Hoot and Pericles to amuse each other by chatting away. When nobody was looking, I tiptoed away. I sneaked off when nobody was looking because I wanted to have a look round for places where Pericles may have hidden our Time Machine.

Doctor Hoot seemed so enthralled by finding out all about the Ancient Greeks that he didn't have time to think about how sad he would be if he never got to see his family or friends again. And I know that Doctor Hoot would be very sad indeed if he never got to see his favourite television show, Eastenders, again.

I searched and searched, but I couldn't find where he had hidden it. I knew that I had to get back to Pericles and the Doctor before I was missed. But all of the time that I was with them I knew that I would be wracking my brains to think where he had put our machine!

At the end of the docks was a magnificent ship. It was called a Trireme and it was huge. There were three rows of oars and an incredible figurehead on the end, made out of metal. I suppose you are wondering what that was for.

Well, it was for something not very nice. The idea, from what I gather, was that the ships would set out and try and go as fast as possible and aim at the enemy ships. They used to ram into the enemy ships and try to sink them before they themselves were sunk. Once all the people were in the water splashing around, fighting for their lives, the archers would come forward with their bows and arrows, and shoot the people in the water. Now that's not very friendly, is it?

Luckily, it didn't look like a war was about to happen, so the Doctor and I weren't going to be asked to take part. Instead we went back to town. I was still interested in the shops.

I suppose you're wondering what the money was like. Well, it was weird. It had pictures of lots of different people on it, but not famous Kings and Queens. At this time in Ancient Greece, they didn't have Kings and Queens. No, they just had a government at that time pretty much run by Pericles, whereas we have got both a government and a monarch.

As they didn't have a King or Queen to put on their coins, they decided to put pictures of Gods on them. Yes, there

was one with Zeus on, there was one with
Athena on, one with Ares on and one with
Poseidon on. Incredible. If you ever see an
Ancient Greek coin and it has 449 BC as its
date, I can tell you that it is a fake. Do you
know how I can tell it is a fake? If you are
very clever, you could work out the reason.
If you are not as clever as me, don't be too

upset because not very many people are as clever as me. I have the kind of wisdom that only comes from being a seasoned time traveller. If you haven't worked out yet how I know that such a coin would be fake then I will tell you. BC stands for Before Christ. Before Christ was born, nobody knew that one day we would use BC and AD as a way of recording time. If you managed to work that out all by yourself before I told you, then you are very clever indeed. I could have done with somebody like you to be with me during my journey to Ancient Greece because you could have helped me to look for my Time Machine.

Well, we decided they must have had a God for everything. They had a God of War, a God of Peace, a God of Music, a God of the Sun, a God of Shepherds; there was also a Goddess of the Fireplace. I know it sounds quite weird, the God of the Fire, but, of course, fire was very important to the Greeks. If your fire went out, you didn't have anything to cook with, light a light or keep yourself warm. Yes, they had about a dozen or so major Gods. Apollo, the God of Music and the Sun, and Hestia, the Goddess of the Fireplace. Ares, of course, was the God of War.

I must be the luckiest time travelling detective in the world. I had arrived in Ancient Greece, taken in all the views, visited a war ship, tried on armour, visited a shoe shop, met famous people like Pericles and, oh, I could stay here forever. No, I couldn't, that's, of course, what Pericles wanted me to do. He had hidden the Time Machine and we could be trapped here forever. The Doctor was looking a bit worried. Better reassure him, I thought, and I had better tell him that I am sure something will turn up and we will find our way home.

As I walked around, I noticed there were loads of girls around, but not many boys. I wondered where all the boys had gone. Have you got any idea? Well, I am afraid only the boys went to school in those days. Yes, girls didn't have to go to school and, what's worse, school started at 5 o'clock every morning. They finished about 2 o'clock in the afternoon, but that's still about 9 hours of school.

School in those days was quite different to our schools today. First of all, you had someone to walk you to school. I know your mum or dad might walk you to school, but this person was a slave called a Pedagogue. His job was to make sure you got to school safely, carry all of your school equipment - basically a musical instrument and something to write on - but, also, his job was to punish you if you misbehaved at school. Yes, if you started messing around at the back of the class, the teacher would give your Pedagogue a nod and he would be able to hit you. I don't think that was very nice, was it? Can you imagine having a Pedagogue sitting next to you all day at school? Someone who gave you a clip round the ear every time you did something naughty! Wow! How horrible would that be? I bet you're glad that you're at school in the twenty first century, aren't you?

At school, children did lessons like they do nowadays, such as maths and a

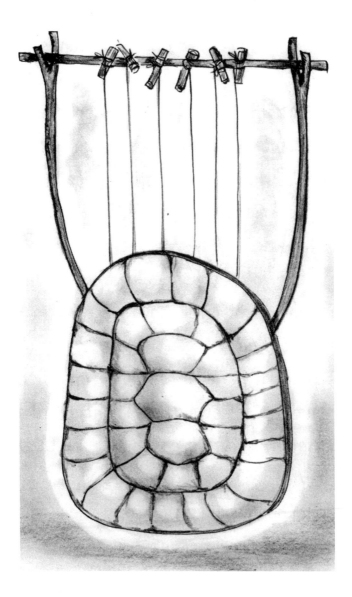

bit of writing, but they also learnt how to talk out loudly. I know that sounds odd, but they were basically being trained to become politicians, a bit like Pericles. So if they could read out poetry and stories loudly in front of a lot of people, they could become as powerful and influential as Pericles was.

I bet you are wondering what the girls were doing while the boys were having all the fun at school.

Well, they were at home. No, they weren't sitting around eating chocolate and watching the TV, which is what the Doctor thought they might be doing. No, they were at home being taught by their mums. Being taught how to cook, how to clean, how to sew, how to wash, how to look after the house. Even though they were in charge of

all those dirty household jobs, if they had slaves they could be more like managers of a hotel, telling the slaves to do all of those jobs. They would be working all day, cooking all sorts of things like, well, lots of fish of course, squid, which I think tastes a bit like rubber bands, olives (I think you either like or hate those), and even making wine. I will tell you about that in a bit.

While the boys were at school, learning how to speak loudly and read and count and even learn how to take part in the Olympic Games (basically doing sports, a bit like your sports day), the girls were at home learning all of the household jobs and things like that. Talking of households, we thought we'd better have a look at Pericles' house. He was more than keen enough to invite us into his home. He, of course, believed I was the Goddess Athena. He would be honoured to have a God visiting his humble house.

It wasn't that humble, it was quite huge. Loads of rooms just like you might have at home. An upstairs and downstairs, a courtyard in the middle. There was a well in one room and even a separate room with a toilet in it. Not like our toilet, though, I am afraid. No, it was basically a big hole in the floor. Yes. And after a few weeks, once it was full up, one of the lucky slaves would be given the job of emptying it. Eee, now that doesn't sound very nice. And I think that it would be jolly smelly too, don't you? Thankfully, the poor slave who had to take all of the human waste away never had to do it whilst I was there. If you think that you are lucky to go to school in the twenty first century, I bet you feel very fortunate indeed that you weren't a slave in Ancient Greece. Even though they were treated quite well by their masters, they still had to work hard and they sometimes had to do jobs that were not terribly nice.

Well, we sat down with Pericles and the rest of his friends, the Doctor and I, and we all had a party. I say sat down, but we actually lay down. They didn't really have many chairs. Everyone lay around on sofas eating their food. The other thing I noticed was there weren't any women there. Yes, girls weren't allowed to go to school, and they also weren't allowed to go to parties. They had the odd dancing girl there but really it was a blokes' thing. Dancing girls were not at the party to enjoy themselves. They were there to entertain men. All the men sitting around, talking about what they had done that day and eating all that beautiful food I mentioned and also drinking wine. Now the wine was... how shall I describe it? Interesting. Yes, it was interesting because you never knew what you might find in it! Your mum and dad might drink wine. Maybe your aunt or uncle. But this wine, I don't think they'd want to drink.

It was made of grapes just like today's wine is, but instead of a big machine squashing the grapes to make the juice, some of the slaves used their feet to squash it in a big wooden bath. Yes, imagine what ended up in that wine. Bits of toenails, bits of skin, corns, hairs, verrucas - you wouldn't get me drinking sweaty feet wine!

They, of course, tried to strain out most of the lumps and even when they poured it into the cup you drink from, they strained it through a big metal spoon with holes in. But still, I wouldn't want to risk it. Think of it, sweaty feet wine, eeeehhh!!

Now if the girls were feeling left out, they were allowed in to the party at the end of the night to maybe have a bit of sweaty feet wine, umm, yes, please! And also to take part in the party game called Kottabos. Sounds a little unusual, doesn't it, Kottabos. Sounds like an aftershave for men.

But, this game involved you throwing a bit of your sweaty feet wine at a target to see who could get the closest. Now, the target wasn't like a dartboard. No, they put a big stick in the ground, balanced a coin on the top, and your job was to try and knock the coin off the top. If you managed to do it, you'd probably get to keep the coin and it showed that you were a very honest person and probably the most faithful to your boyfriend or girlfriend. The Ancient Greeks believed that being able to hit a target was a very desirable trait in a human being. They believed that if your aim was true then you were a truthful person.

Well, one of the guests at the party, Pericles' daughter, had taken a shine to me. Yes, Doctor Hoot kept nudging me and saying, "Oh, she keeps looking at you!"

I tried to look the other way. I think she was quite keen on me. So when it was my go to have a game at Kottabos, I deliberately missed, so that she couldn't say that I was keen on her too.

As they sat there, drinking more and more sweaty feet wine, they were getting sillier and sillier. They kept shouting, "Athena, Athena, Athena." Yes, the more they drank, the more they believed I was the Goddess Athena.

I kept telling them, "I'm not Athena."

I kept shouting. But the more I shouted, the more they believed I was.

As we sat there thinking that these people believed I was the Goddess Athena, the Doctor had a brilliant idea.

The Doctor said, "You know they think you're a God?"

"Yes," I said.

"Well, Gods aren't supposed to do anything wrong are they?"

"No, you're right there," I said.

"Well, if you do something really, really wrong, then that would prove to them you're not a God."

"What a brilliant idea," I said, "but what could I do?"

"Well," he said. "I've heard in the streets that the Olympic Games starts tomorrow. If you take part in the Olympic Games," he says, "and really, really, really mess it up, and lose in a really, really bad way, that will prove to them you're not the Goddess Athena."

"What a fan dabby bostin' idea," I thought. I was always rubbish at sport at school, so it should be no problem losing the Olympic Games.

We went to sleep that night on a really uncomfortable bed. Pretty much a wooden box with a straw-filled mattress. Not like our nice comfy beds. But I dreamt of the plan the Doctor had created. Me losing the Olympic Games.

When I woke up in the morning, I quietly sneaked out of the house to look for our Time Machine. It was no use, though. I couldn't find it anywhere. I knew that Pericles was a very clever man. After all, he was the most important man in all of Ancient Greece. But I just kept on wondering where on earth he could have hidden my Time Machine.

The next day the sun was out as hot as ever. It was baking hot. Even though their houses only had small windows, I still felt I was getting cooked, it was so warm. We headed off down to the Olympic stadium of Olympia next to the Temple of Zeus. I suppose it looked a bit like one of our football stadiums, though not as big, and, instead of a football pitch or grass, they just had a sort of sandy track.

All the people there were training for their events. The crowds were quite exciteable. I could tell that this was rather an important time. They had events like we've got at our Olympics nowadays: people throwing various things as far as they could, people jumping as high as they could, people running as fast as they could. And the event I was chosen to take part in first of all, was the javelin. Basically throwing a big spear as far as you could. But when I saw people warming up to take part, I had rather a shock. They had no clothes on! Can you believe that? There were grown men running around with no clothes on. They were in the nuddy! Stark naked! Can you imagine that? How would you like to be running and throwing things around with lots of people looking at you? Yes, well, that's how it felt. I told Doctor Hoot that I wouldn't do it. I told him that it was altogether undignified. But Doctor Hoot told me that I should do it. He told me that we were in Ancient Greece now and we should act like Ancient Greeks. I told him that I couldn't possibly go out into the middle of a huge stadium with no clothes on! It's not right! It's not proper. It's not what people should do. When you're having a bath, that's the time to be in the nuddy. Not when you're doing the long jump. But Doctor Hoot said that the Ancient Greeks thought that the human body was beautiful and that it was a nice thing to show people how beautiful you are. In fact, the Olympic Games in Greece were not all about who could run the fastest. The way they looked when they ran was more important than how fast they could run. Some judges were assembled from the upper classes of society and they would watch the race and between them they would decide who looked the best when they were running and that would be the winner. Once I stopped to think about it, I realised there is nothing rude about the human body. It's just a matter of what we think is right for our times. After all, the Victorians would think it very odd to see people walking around the beach the way we do today because they thought that such behaviour was inappropriate. I decided that if I was to be a time traveller, I had to learn to accept that I would need to do some things that may not be part of our culture today.

Well, the first competitor grabbed hold of his javelin and stepped up to the launching line. The crowd were screaming. He was obviously very popular. He threw his javelin as far as he could. It looked like it went a mile. The next competitor threw it even further. And then it was my turn. I picked up the javelin and stepped forward. The Doctor gave me a knowing wink from the audience where he was standing, letting me know that I should remember to keep losing as much as I could. Okay, I thought, and I threw it about 3 metres in front of me. The crowd all went silent. They were amazed that the Goddess Athena could be so bad at throwing the javelin. Little did they know it was all a big plan. Had that done the trick? Had that made them realise I wasn't really a God? Not at all. The Athenians believed it was all part of a big test that their Goddess Athena was trying to do for them. They believed I was trying to test them to see if they would

try to beat the Goddess Athena.

The second event was the discus. Throwing something else as far as you could, but this time it was a bit like a big stone frisbee. This time they made me go first. I would have to try and be as bad at this as possible. Right, I grabbed hold of my discus, pulled my arm back, the crowd were silent, waiting to see exactly how far I would throw it. And I dropped it on my foot. Yes, that was my throw. I was going to stick with that. I was more than happy with throwing it exactly onto my foot. It hurt a bit. But the next competitor stepped forward and looked a bit pale. You may well wonder how he was going to be worse than me.

Well, he picked up his discus, pulled his arm back and threw it behind him.

They were trying to make me win. They couldn't believe the Goddess Athena would be so bad at sport, so they wanted me to be the best. The third competitor took it home! Oh, this was looking bad. It looked like I was going to be winning the Olympic Games.

This went on the whole time. When I jumped really, really low, everyone else jumped even lower, when, in fact, the event was the high jump. This went on all day until the final event - the 100m sprint. Now normally, of course, you are supposed to run as fast as you can to get to the other end. It should take about 10 seconds if you are really, really fast. Well, we all lined up at the starting line, ready to run it in 10 seconds flat. The starting person shouted "GO" and nobody moved. We all just stood there. The starting person shouted "GO" again. And then "GO, GO, GO" in case we hadn't heard it. We'd heard it all right, but none of us wanted to run. I didn't want to win, and no one else wanted to beat me.

Ooh, we stood there for a good 10 minutes. The crowd looked very confused. I thought I'd better test these Greeks to see how loyal they were to their Goddess Athena. So, I cunningly took a step forward. Immediately, all of the others stepped forward as well, but slightly less than me so they were still behind me but looked like they were trying to compete. I took another step forward. And so did they, but still leaving me just enough in front so I could be called the winner. I took a couple of steps. And sure enough, they followed suit but still remaining behind me to try and make me the winner.

Another 10 minutes went by. We were still no further down the track. I thought I would have a bit of fun with them, so I stepped backwards. Ha ha, this will fool them, I thought. But it didn't. They all stepped backwards as well. There was no way they were going to let me lose this event.

Three hours went by, four hours, most of the people watching had fallen asleep. Some of them had gone home. After about seven hours, the sun started to go down and the person that started the race was thinking of going home for his tea. Well, after seven hours we were almost at the finish line. The Doctor and I realised our plan had really backfired. We would have to think of some other way of getting out of Ancient Greece.

Pericles had stolen the Time Machine, hidden it somewhere where we were never going to find it, and it seemed as if we were

going to be stuck there for ever!

In one final step, I resigned myself to winning the Olympic Games. I stepped over the finish line.

"Athena, Athena," they all shouted.

Their Goddess Athena had beaten everyone else and everyone was relieved. All the other competitors just collapsed on the floor from the exhaustion of not running enough. They picked up me and the Doctor and dragged us all the way back to Pericles' house to celebrate with more sweaty feet wine!

Back at Pericles's house, the whole dining room was set out ready for a party, just like the night before, with big, big vases filled with lots of stinky, sweaty feet wine. Neither of us wanted to sit there drinking wine and eating their really quite nice food again. They had dishes of fish and fruit with meat and olives and dates. I had more important things to worry about. Well, for a start they thought I was the Goddess Athena still and, secondly, I had no way of getting home with the Doctor. Pericles, of course, had stolen the Time Machine, hidden it somewhere where we were never going to find it. And even if I did find it, it was broken. How was I going to mend it?

I wasn't going to find it or mend it sitting around in this dining room filled with sweaty feet wine. So I decided to go and investigate. Well, the Doctor and I managed to slip out through a side door from the dining room and wandered out into the courtyard. Maybe Pericles had hidden the Time Machine somewhere in his

house. Well, it wasn't in the courtyard, it wasn't in that room I told you about which was the, the you know what! Maybe it was upstairs.

Stepping up the wooden steps, I could hear a lot of chattering coming from one end of the corridor. I walked up to the door, opened it and inside, of course, found all the women. Those women that weren't allowed to go to the party. They were busy as anything. They were busy weaving on huge looms, weaving with wool, making, well, all sorts of clothes, I expect. They were weaving clothes for themselves and were also weaving clothes for the men as well. They were very similar. The women's clothes were called Chitons, but spelt with a 'ch', not like kite, but like church. It's basically a big sheet that they folded in

half, wrapped around themselves, put a couple of pins on the shoulders and a belt round the middle. And 'voila', you have got an instantaneous outfit. The men's outfits were pretty much the same. They were sometimes called Peplos, but also called Chitons as well. They were just a bit shorter. I think the Greek men quite liked showing off their legs a bit. I suppose boys tend to show more than girls today, don't they? Maybe they do, maybe they don't, you can decide that for yourself. The important thing to remember is that people always have a lot in common. The things that differ tend to be the way they do things. That is what culture is all about. It might seem odd to you that men in Ancient Greece would wear something that we might think of as a dress today, but that was their culture. They were very sensible things to wear because they were much cooler than the suits men in Britain wear today. They were very practical indeed. They would probably think it very odd to see the way we dress today. Have you ever thought how silly it is that men wear ties? There is absolutely no reason for them whatsoever. They are simply an accessory that men wear to look nice or, to put it another way, wearing a tie is part of our culture. Being a time traveller has taught me never to laugh at the way other people do things. The ways of other people may seem strange to me but my ways will seem strange to them.

Well, these women were busy as anything, like I say, making clothes while their husbands, brothers and boyfriends were downstairs having a good old party. There were lots of women in here, making lots of clothes, but there was no Time Machine. Maybe I'd find it in one of the other rooms.

I went into another room and there was a poor looking boy who was wearing quite rough ragged clothes. I walked over to have a word. His name was Thera, and it turned out that he was a slave. He didn't look that happy but then again he looked pretty well looked after. He began to tell me about some of the work and jobs he had to do around the house. Well, I was amazed. It was pretty much everything from, like I say, cleaning out the toilet, to helping make food, helping with shopping, helping the young boy get to school in the morning. Just about anything, and, if he had any time left in the day, he was allowed to have a bit of a lie down and a rest.

Being a slave in Ancient Greece probably wasn't that nice but there could come a time in your life as a slave when you could be set free, either when your master or mistress died, maybe in his will he could let you free, or you could save up somehow and buy your own freedom.

This young slave boy led us down the stairs to meet his sister. We walked into the kitchen. It looked pretty much like one of our kitchens, lots of pots and pans bubbling away over cookers. Well, fires, really. They were preparing all the food for the greedy men in the dining room. You could tell she was his sister, they looked so alike. She was holding something very strange in her hand. It was something that

I'd seen at one of the schools. Yes, like a wooden board filled with bees' wax. Not ear wax, no. Bees' wax. This is what they used to write on in those days. The Romans were so impressed with the Greeks' invention of these wax boards, that they used them as well.

These wax boards were called Deltions. You basically scratched into the wax using a thing called a Stylus. A Stylus was the name they gave to a big pointy stick. You could write in a Deltion, read it out, take it to the shops with your shopping list written on it. And once you had used it, you could rub out the writing using the other end of the Stylus. Or, if you wanted to rub it out completely, put it on something a bit like a little barbecue. Yes, it really did look like a barbecue, and you heat it up and melt the wax. Quite amazing. I am amazed we don't have them nowadays. It may not be as quick as using a pen or a computer but it is good fun.

Well, I thought we might be missed from the party as Pericles was shouting, "Athena, Athena" from the dining room, so we wandered back. On the way back, I had a chat with the Doctor. He was very, very concerned for a lot of reasons. Firstly, we appeared to be trapped in Ancient Greece. Secondly ,Pericles believed I was a God and the Doctor was my helper. Thirdly, Pericles had hidden the Time Machine somewhere. We didn't know where it was, and even then it was broken. And fourthly, Doctor Hoot had definitely missed that evening's episode of Eastenders. He just hoped that we'd be back for Saturday when he could go to the local football match. Did I tell you he was a big Birmingham United fan? Or is it Birmingham City? I can never remember. I think it's a rather silly game. Lots of people rush around a field kicking a ball. I don't see the point of it. I wonder what the Ancient Greeks would have made of it? Of course, I couldn't tell Pericles about the future. If I were to tell them about something that hadn't yet been invented, that could change the whole course of history and I didn't want to be responsible for that! I do think that it would have been fun, though, to tell them all about Manchester United and Chelsea and all of the other teams. They would probably have thought that I was mad. Do you see how people may seem odd if they do things that are part of their culture but not of yours? It doesn't mean that they are really odd. It just means that they are different.

Ahh, he only thinks of himself!

Back in the dining room, Pericles and his friends were all lounging around, tucking into the sweaty feet wine, when he claimed he had a great idea. He, of course, believed I was the Goddess Athena and, where better to take a visiting God than to the theatre. That was the first place we'd wanted to go before all these bizarre happenings had taken place. We had wanted to go to the theatre when we first arrived and now Pericles, the person that was keeping us in Greece, wanted to take us there. We'd have to wait till the next day before we could go and visit the theatre.

As I sat there on my uncomfortable bed for the second night in a row, I started thinking of all the nice things the Greeks had done. Yes, even though they'd kept us prisoner and not let the Doctor get home for his precious TV and football, they had been really, really nice. They had got great jobs, great looking weapons. They'd got reasonably nice food, except for the sweaty feet wine, and everyone was pretty much really pleasant. Well, I'd heard of some other Greek people that weren't, some people called Spartans, yes. We still use the word Spartan nowadays to describe something that's sort of not very comfortable and not very generous.

Yes, the Spartans were horrible people. They lived in the south of Ancient Greece. They do really bad things. If a baby had been born in the town and he didn't look that well, the mother and father would take the baby to the elders who ran the town, show the baby to them and sometimes the elders would get the baby, well, put the baby on the side of a mountain and say that if it survived the

night, they could keep the baby. Now, I am not suggesting that any of you do that with your baby brother or sister, because it is a horrible thing to do. They were really dreadful.

Whereas the Athenians, from the age of seven, went to school to learn reading, writing, counting, poetry, art and sculpture, the Spartans were training for war. Yes, they were ready for battle at all times. Ahh, I suppose the Ancient Athenians were as well. Their Olympic Games and practising sport at school wasn't so they could train to become great sportsmen. That was training them to become good fighters and warriors too. Throwing the javelin was basically learning how to throw a spear at the enemy. But at least they weren't throwing spears at me and, for

the moment, they were treating me pretty nicely as it was.

Well, the next morning came and it seemed to be even hotter than the one before. We stepped outside, heading towards the theatre. The streets were filled with people, all flocking on their way to the theatre. It was obviously a very important play that was going to be on. And in the streets, I noticed the children playing with some unusual toys.

When I look out of my window back at home in modern times, I can see children playing on scooters, playing with all sorts of electronic toys and modern gadgets, but in those days they played with lots of clay toys. Little clay figures of cows and horses, and spinning tops, that kind of thing. They seemed to be enjoying themselves, even though they didn't have the luxury of having the modern up-to- date electronic toys you get at home.

We headed up the streets, straight to the theatre. The theatre looked almost familiar. Yes, our theatres have got lots of banks of seats sloping up to the sides, almost in a semi-circle in a way. Well, they're based on Ancient Greek theatres. The Greeks realised that was the best shape to have for a theatre. The stage

down at the bottom and the seats leading all the way up to the top at the sides because, well, for two reasons. Firstly, everyone in the audience can see what is going on on the stage, and also, everyone can hear what's going on. If you whispered down on the stage, someone right on the back row at the top of the theatre could hear what you were saying.

Well, Pericles was there. He wasn't letting me out of his sight. He was still convinced, of course, that I was the Goddess Athena. He still hadn't told us where he'd hidden the Time Machine and he was still making sure we weren't out of his sight.

We all sat down for a moment. But, strangely enough, only I was allowed to sit down on the front row. I later found out that the front row was reserved for Gods. You may think that this is the silliest thing that you have ever heard but the whole front row of the theatre, all of the seats, were left completely empty so that if a God came to visit, they'd have somewhere to sit. How strange! Also what was strange was the fact that everyone in the town seemed to be there. At parties, it was just the men. At executive parties, it was only the rich men. But the theatre had rich men, poor men, also women, children, all sorts of poor people and even slaves. If you couldn't afford a ticket to go to the theatre, the rich people would buy you one. What a great idea, and the theatre was a real chance to meet various people from the town that normally you wouldn't be allowed to socialise with. The theatre was the great social gathering. It was the one social occasion that allowed people from all over the city to meet together, and for this reason it became the most talked about thing in Greece. If you meet up with friends you would probably talk about a film that you had seen or a football match that you had been to. That is certainly the kind of thing that Doctor Hoot talks about. Birmingham, Birmingham, Birmingham or Eastenders, Eastenders, Eastenders. That's what he usually goes on about. Well, when the Doctor and I listened to people talking in Ancient Greece, all they talked about was theatre, theatre, theatre.

Pericles ran over.

"I must introduce you to this person," he said.

This old man with a long white beard,

not looking dissimilar to Father Christmas, walked over.

"Who on earth are you?" I asked.

"My name is Sophocles," he said.

"Sophocles, I know that name," I thought.

Yes, Sophocles was a famous playwright. He wrote some great plays in Greece, not very funny, no, he didn't write any of the comedies, I am afraid. He only wrote the tragedies. Those were the two main sorts of plays in Ancient Greece. We think of comedies as being something that makes us laugh today but that wasn't the case in Ancient Greece. Comedies tended to be more pleasant than tragedies. This was because they had a happy ending. It was the happy ending that made it a comedy. If the main character or all the

main characters died at the end of a play then that play would be called a tragedy. Sophocles was the writer of the play we were about to see. But he had a surprise in store for us.

I was very interested to hear what Sophocles had to say. I went for a drink of sweaty feet wine with Sophocles and his friends. Before Sophocles told me about his plan, his friends mentioned something about the Gods. This was to prove to be just about the best part of our entire visit. They mentioned a story about the Gods that involved Athena. Well, of course, the Doctor and I were delighted to hear about this and we wanted to hear more. Sophocles and our new friends were delighted to tell us more.

That day, I listened to the most

amazing story that I had ever heard.  It started with Nyriads.

Nyriads were the immortal nymphs of the sea.  A gorgeous one was called Thetis. Thetis was particularly well known among Nyriads because the King of the Gods fell in love with her. You may have heard of the King of the Gods. His name was Zeus.  For human beings, it would be great for a King to fall in love with a girl because she would become a Queen.  I bet most girls, if they were really honest, would say that they would love to fall in love with a Prince so that they could become a Princess.  Then, when the Prince becomes King, she would become Queen.

Thetis was not very keen on the idea of Zeus falling in love with her, though. She did not welcome his attention for two reasons.

The first reason was the most important. Zeus was already married! He was married to Hera. And what made it worse was that Hera was Thetis's stepmother. Can you believe the cheek of him? I know he was the King of the Gods, but, honestly! Fancy asking your wife's stepdaughter to marry you!

They told me that stories about the Greek Gods were the best stories ever, but I'm not sure that I was expecting that. But, to be honest, that was just the beginning. The story of the Trials of Paris turned out to be just about one of the best stories that I had ever heard. Even Doctor Hoot listened with his beak open.

"You know," he told me. "I think the stories of the Greek Gods are even better than the stories in Eastenders."

When Thetis told Zeus that she would not marry him, he was very angry indeed. One of the main differences between Gods and Mortals was that Gods normally got their own way. They weren't like Mortals who generally have to put up with things the way they are. If you were a God, you got very angry if things were not just the way that you wanted them to be. If you were Zeus, King of the Gods, then you wanted everything your own way.

Zeus decided to get his revenge.

"If Thetis won't marry me," he grumbled, "then she will never marry any Immortal. She will have to marry a Human instead of a God. That will be her punishment."

Well, that was a very cruel punishment indeed. Human beings don't enjoy the special powers that Gods have. And this cruel punishment was all because Thetis would not marry the God that was already married to her stepmother, Hera! Actually, I said there were two reasons why she would not marry him. The second reason was that Zeus was old and rather stout and he had a long grey beard. Thetis was young and beautiful. The thought of the two of them being all lovey dovey and all kissy kissy was a horrible thought for Thetis.

Soon the word went out among all the sea nymphs that Thetis was going to have to marry a Mortal. All of the other sea nymphs were a little jealous of Thetis because she was the most beautiful and gorgeous of them all. When they found out that her punishment for refusing to marry Zeus was that she had to marry a Mortal, they began to tease Thetis.

"Thetis has to marry a Mortal. Thetis has to marry a Mortal," they chanted at her.

As you can imagine, this made Thetis very sad.

She went to her stepmother, Hera, and told her how sad she was. Hera was a kind stepmother. She knew she could do nothing to change the punishment that Zeus had given to her, but she decided to make sure that she would find the very best of the Mortals so that she could put a smile back on her stepdaughter's face.

Hera chose a King. His name was Peleus. He was handsome and young. Thetis could see herself being all lovey dovey kissy kissy with someone young and handsome, but it did not matter how young and handsome

Peleus was, he was still a Human.

"I have chosen King Peleus for you," Hera told Thetis. "He has a magic sword!"

Thetis' mood brightened. Now that tickled her fancy. A Mortal with a magic sword! The sound of that made her think that being all lovey dovey kissy kissy with him didn't sound so bad at all.

"What magic can it do, then?" Thetis asked her stepmother.

She had dreams of Peleus being as powerful, or even more powerful, than many Immortals that she could have married.

"Well," said Hera. "The magic in the sword means that he can win any fight that he gets into."

"Is that all?" Thetis asked. "Is that all the magic his sword can do? That's no use to me! I won't marry him if that's all the magic he has!"

Hera was disappointed in her stepdaughter.

"I'm sorry, Thetis," she told her, "the marriage has already been arranged."

Well, the next thing that happened in this story was fifty thousand times better than anything you would ever see on Eastenders. When they told us the next part of the story, I thought Doctor Hoot was going to faint! He ducked from side to side and backwards and forwards as though all of the things that were happening in the story were happening to him!

Thetis was so furious at the thought of having to marry a Mortal that she ran away. Well, being a water nymph, she didn't have to run. She took off on the back of a dolphin and he made his way through the water as if his life depended on it. In very little time at all, she reached a secluded island where she planned to rest for a while and think about her life.

Soon, though, she found that she was not alone. No. Peleus was there. He was the happiest Human alive when he found out he was going to marry an Immortal. He was waiting for Thetis because he wanted

more than anything to marry her. He did not know that she did not want to marry him. He wanted to be all lovey dovey kissy kissy but Thetis was having none of it.

Now, this is something that you don't get on Eastenders. To get away from Peleus, Thetis turned herself into fire. Peleus was so determined that Thetis should be his wife that he was not put off by this. He hung on for dear life. And even though he was burned in the struggle, he would not let go.

So then Thetis turned herself into water, but he still wouldn't let go. So she turned herself into a huge lion with a massive mane and the biggest, sharpest teeth that you have ever seen. And her roar was the most frightening and ferocious roar that Peleus had ever heard. But he was so determined that the beautiful Thetis should be his wife that still he wouldn't let go.

Then Thetis turned herself into a snake. A long snake with dark eyes and a forked tongue. But still Peleus held on for all his worth. She even turned herself into an octopus with tentacles flying around her. Although Peleus was very tired, still he hung on with grim determination.

Do you know what? Peleus was no fool. Most Mortals would have just given in and taken "no" for an answer, but, because Peleus wasn't like most Mortals, Thetis began to have second thoughts. She began to think that maybe Hera was right after all. If Peleus was so determined that being burned, drenched, roared at, squeezed by a snake and being squirted by octopus ink

would not make him give in, then maybe he was worth marrying after all. Thetis began to think of him in a new light. The thought of being all lovey dovey kissy kissy with him seemed quite a nice thought after all.

The whole world had never seen a wedding quite like the wedding of the Mortal King Peleus and the Immortal Nyriad nymph, Thetis. Everybody was there. Mortals and Immortals attended the wedding side by side. The wedding took place in the cooling air of an Athens evening. The nine Muses sang the most beautiful of choruses to fill the darkening skies, and the ceremony was backlit by a full moon and a sprinkling of stars. Centaurs cantered back and forth with Nereids riding upon them. Hera was delighted for her stepdaughter, and Zeus, who had recently been very grumpy indeed,

had warmed to the union. Zeus and Hera sat beside each other and were indeed pleased to see Peleus and Thetis so happy together.

Normally, you would only ever see Doctor Hoot upset if Birmingham City were losing a football match, or if he couldn't get to see Eastenders maybe, but even he was moved by the story of Peleus and Thetis getting married. I'm not sure that I saw him cry, though. I'm not sure if owls can cry. Anyway, I do know that Doctor Hoot does like a good yarn and he told me that hearing this story was the best part of his visit to Ancient Greece. Doctor Hoot and I sat very still while we waited for the next instalment of the story.

Well, it was not just Peleus and Thetis who were feeling lovey dovey kissy kissy.

All around, Mortals and Immortals alike were holding hands and looking into each other's eyes. It looked very much as though everybody was feeling very lovey dovey kissy kissy.

One uninvited guest changed all that, though. Her name was Eris and she was not the kind of God that anyone would want to invite to their wedding. She was exceedingly unpleasant to look at. She had bony arms and bony hands and she had a bony face that had long straggly hair hung all around it. Her teeth were dark and her eyes were darker still.

As the wedding guests came to realise that Eris had arrived, the music and happy chatter died away to silence. Eris slowly moved her head around to make sure that everybody was looking at her and then she

took an apple from an old cloth sack. It was no ordinary apple, though. It was a golden apple. It shone so brightly in the full moonlight that a gulp could be heard from all therepresent. She rolled the apple down the slight hill in front of her and then she gave out a cruel wicked cry and faded into the background where she disappeared.

The golden apple fell at the feet of three Gods who were huddled together like witches. The first God was the Goddess Hera, and the other two were Athena, the Goddess of Wisdom, and Aphrodite, the Goddess of Love.

Hera said to Peleus, "Go on, pick up the apple!"

Peleus was a little bit reluctant to pick it up. It seemed to have a strange, eerie quality about it, and no Mortal would take anything from Eris without being just a little bit concerned, because, as you will no doubt remember, she is the Goddess of Strife and Discord. But, because Hera was the stepmother of his beautiful new bride, and because she was a God and he was a Mortal, he did as he was told and picked up the golden apple.

Holding the apple had a draining effect on him. He suddenly felt weak, as though he had bad 'flu, and he had a headache and his hands started to shake. There was some writing on the apple which told Peleus who he should give the apple to.

It said, "Give this apple to the fairest of the three Goddesses before you."

Athena, Hera and Aphrodite were all very keen to see which of them Peleus thought was the fairest.

"Are you going to give me the apple?" Athena asked Peleus.

"Give it to me, Peleus, please!" Hera said.

"Will you choose me?" asked Aphrodite.

Poor Peleus didn't know who he should give it to. He knew that whichever decision he made would be the wrong one. Have you ever seen two naughty children fighting in the playground and a circle of even naughtier children gather round them to see what they were doing? Well, that's just how it was here. All the guests gathered round to see who Peleus was going to choose because everybody knew that the two Goddesses who weren't chosen would be very angry indeed.

The situation was a party stopper and no mistake. Peleus's mouth was really dry. He thought about reaching for a glass of sweaty feet wine, but, with everybody looking at him, he was too frightened to move. His eyes met Hera's and he wished he was back wrestling a lion. And when he looked at Athena and Aphrodite, they looked even more frightening still.

Zeus stepped in to help Peleus.

"Look," he said. "Tonight is a night for celebration. Everybody will go back to doing what they were doing before the apple turned their heads. We will not decide tonight who shall be given the apple. We will leave that decision until another day. And, anyway, Peleus just picked the apple up. It doesn't mean that it has to be Peleus that makes the decision."

Athena, the Goddess of Wisdom, was immediately concerned that Zeus was planning to make the decision himself.

"You can't choose," she told him. "You're bound to choose Hera because she is your wife and that wouldn't be fair."

Aphrodite agreed with Athena and told Zeus that it would not be fair if he chose. They caught Zeus in a good mood. His recent grumpiness had left him. Along with all the other guests, he was feeling quite lovey dovey kissy kissy, so he decided that a man would make the decision. Zeus took the golden apple from Peleus, who was delighted to be rid of it. He shook his free hands and reached out to hug Thetis. Zeus spoke.

"The decision will be made by Paris, son of Priam," he declared.

The darkest hour of the night descended upon the wedding guests and they began to drift away. The party was over.

"I don't think there will ever be an episode of Eastenders with Kings, Queens, Gods and Goddesses in it," Doctor Hoot said.

"Who was Paris, son of Priam?" I asked.

Neither of us could wait to find out what Paris was like, and what he would do with the golden apple.

Well, Priam and Hecuba were the King and Queen of Troy. When Hecuba was expecting Paris, she had the most dreadful dream. It was a nightmare. It was so bad that it woke her up and it frightened her so much that she couldn't sleep for a long time.

If you have ever had a nightmare then you will know how frightening they can be. If you had a nightmare as frightening as this one, you would probably never want to sleep again. She dreamt that when her baby was born, she went to look at him the way new mothers do, but her baby wasn't a baby at all - it was a blazing log! She screamed and couldn't believe what she was seeing and she rubbed her eyes and looked again. This time there were sparks coming from the burning log and worms were crawling from it. Long red, fiery worms. Hecuba woke from her bad dream, and she had been sweating and screaming in her sleep. Priam was heartbroken for his poor wife and he hugged and cuddled her to try and calm her down. But it was no use. No matter how much Priam gave to her, she couldn't stop trembling and shaking and crying.

Priam went to consult with a seer. It was a very common thing for people in Ancient Greece to consult seers. People would make very important decisions about their lives based on the advice of seers. It was a bit like people in our lifetime who look at their star signs in the newspaper, but when people do that today, it is mostly seen as a bit of fun. In Ancient Greece, visiting a seer was a very serious business indeed.

Priam went to the seer and told him about his wife's dream.

"This is a very serious dream indeed," the seer told him, gravely. "The baby your wife is expecting will grow up to destroy Troy. If you want to save your country, then you must kill the baby as soon as he is born. Otherwise, not only will your son destroy Troy, but he will also destroy the rest of your family as well. You must kill your newborn baby or tens of thousands of your citizens will die and so will all your other children. If he lives all this will come to pass. Mark my words."

This news was the worst news that King Priam could have been given. How could he kill his own son? How could any father kill his own son? But the thought that thousands of his people would die if he didn't was a dreadful one. He also kept thinking about his other children. The thought that they would all die because he didn't kill his newborn made him very sad indeed.

This was an awful dilemma. Priam had sleepless night after sleepless night until his son was born.

The newborn son was Paris.  King Priam had decided that Paris must die to save the rest of his family and all of Troy.  But when the King looked at his newborn son, he knew that he could not kill him.  Still, he knew that he must die, so he decided to give that awful job to someone else.  He called for his chief shepherd and told him to do this dreadful deed.

The chief shepherd was very upset to be given such a job.  If any other person in Troy had given him such a job, he would certainly have refused.  But this was no ordinary person telling him to do this.  This person was his King. The King of Troy. He wasn't the kind of man that was refused anything.

With a heavy heart, he took the child

off into the mountains. But when he got there, he could not summon up the strength to put his sword through the body of the small baby. He decided instead that he would leave the child to perish. He left the child on the mountainside and went back down to his village. He knew that a small baby could not survive without his mother. He also knew that the hot Greek days and the cold Greek nights would make it impossible for the boy to survive. He told himself that it would be better that way. He told himself that, in this way, he wasn't killing the child, he was simply not keeping him alive. He knew in his heart, though, that what he was doing was a very dreadful thing indeed.

When seven days and seven nights had passed, the shepherd went back to the mountainside to collect the body of the dead child.  But, to his great surprise, he found that the child wasn't dead at all.  He was well fed and seemed to be well looked after and very happy indeed.  The child must have been cared for by wild animals. There was no other explanation for it.  The shepherd drew his sword to complete the task that he should have completed a week ago, but, when he looked down at the baby's smiling face, his heart melted.  The boy was beautiful and he had a bonny smiling face.

It was no good.  He knew that he could never take his sword to the child, no matter how hard he tried.  The poor shepherd sobbed and cried.  He knew that he could never face Priam and tell him that he had failed to carry out his orders.  The shepherd decided that he would take the boy home and raise him as his own son. This he did. He told the King that his child had been killed. The King was sad about this awful thing that he had done, but he told himself that he had done it for his country and for the rest of his family.

Paris grew up to be a fine boy. He had bright eyes and he was bigger, stronger, faster and much cleverer than any other child. The shepherd was a good father, and Paris was a good son who made his father very proud of him. Paris grew up to be a shepherd who was every bit as good as his father.

Well, at this point, Doctor Hoot and I looked at each other and I blinked. We had been so transfixed by this story that I don't think either of us had moved a muscle. This was the best story that we had ever been told and we were both very eager indeed to find out what happened next.

One day, when Paris was out on the hills tending his father's sheep, he had the most amazing visitors. The three Goddesses, Hera, Athena and Aphrodite came to see him and they had with them Hermes, the messenger of the Gods.

Hermes was a God who had wings. He hovered around Paris for a while and settled before him. Paris was startled. He had no idea that he was really a Prince. He had lived as an ordinary shepherd boy and a visit from a God was a great shock to him.

"I have come with a message from Zeus, the King of the Gods," Hermes told Paris.

He gave Paris the golden apple that had been left by Eris.

"This apple must be given to the fairest of these three Goddesses. Zeus has decreed that it is you, Paris, that must choose."

Paris was very clever, and he knew it would be a huge mistake to anger any Goddess. He thought for a moment.

"I know," he said. "Let's cut the apple into three equal pieces and share it among all three of you."

"You are very clever," Hermes congratulated Paris, "but the orders from Zeus are clear. You must choose which Goddess is the fairest and give the whole apple to her. If you wish to please Zeus, you must follow his orders."

Hera had found out that Paris very much liked to have girlfriends. She knew that he liked to be all lovey dovey kissy

kissy, so she appeared to him as a beautiful young woman. Her hair was gorgeous and she had beautiful makeup and jewellery.

"Choose me, Paris," she advised. "For I am Zeus's wife and I sit beside him on Mount Olympus. Were you to make an enemy of me, I could be very dangerous indeed."

She was not joking. She had turned one enemy into a ball of fire and she had turned another into a cow! When Hercules crossed her, she set about ruining his life so badly that he eventually went out of his mind!

But she didn't only threaten Paris.

"If you choose me," she went on, "your reward will be very great. I will make you the most powerful lord in Asia. I will make you richer than the King of Troy. In fact, I will be so grateful, that I will make you the richest man in the whole wide world."

"Well," remarked Doctor Hoot. "Who could resist that? He is bound to choose her now. No Mortal would want to make an enemy of the wife of Zeus."

I agreed with him and I told him that there were not many shepherd boys who would give up the chance of being the richest Human in all the world. But then Athena appeared to him.

Now I already know quite a lot about Athena because, as I told you, that's who Pericles believed that I was. But as they told me the story, there were a few new things that I found out about her. As well as being the Goddess of Wisdom, she was also sometimes the Goddess of War. That was something for Paris to think about, because it may be a very big mistake indeed for a Mortal to make an enemy of the Goddess of War. When Paris heard about this, he kept thinking about Hera being the wife of Zeus, but what he heard next about Athena really made him think again.

Athena was actually Zeus's daughter. She was the daughter of Zeus and his first wife, Metis. You've probably heard the story of Little Red Riding Hood and the granny who was swallowed by the wolf. Well, Zeus was a bit like that. When his wife, Metis, annoyed him, he swallowed her whole and then Athena was born out of his mouth!

Doctor Hoot turned to me and said, "You don't get storylines like that in Eastenders, do you?"

And even though I don't watch Eastenders all of the time, I was fairly certain that he was right!

Athena set about persuading Paris to choose her as the fairest of the three Goddesses.

"Paris, if you choose me, I will make you the wisest man in all the world. Great wisdom is worth much more than great wealth."

She told him that to give him such a gift was within her powers as the Goddess of Wisdom. But she also told him that, as she had been the Goddess of War, she could make him a great warrior.

"How would you feel if you knew that you would never ever lose a battle? You would be invincible!"

Athena was very tense when she was

talking to Paris. She did not take to him much. She knew about his fondness for girlfriends and she knew that he liked to be all lovey dovey kissy kissy. Athena was not like that. She believed that being wise was far more important than all of that. She reminded Paris that she had given the world the ability to weave, she had invented the pottery wheel, she had taught human beings how to tame horses and she had shown them how to make the first chariots. She again told him to choose her as the fairest and reminded him that wisdom was far more important than anything.

Doctor Hoot turned to speak to me again. I think that he was quite worried for Paris. He told me that he didn't think any Mortal should make an enemy of the daughter of Zeus. I agreed with him. But if he chose Athena so as not to upset her, then that would mean he was not choosing Hera and that would upset her. I felt sorry for Paris as well. He had an awful dilemma to face. I'm glad I wasn't in that position. I couldn't wait to find out what Aphrodite was going to say to him. Neither could Doctor Hoot. He said that waiting to find out what happened next in this story was worse than waiting to find out what was going to happen in a really good episode of Eastenders. Then Aphrodite appeared to Paris.

The most important thing that you need to know about Aphrodite is that she is the Goddess of Love. Yes, she is the Goddess of all things to do with lovey dovey kissy kissy. So you can imagine that Paris was drawn to Aphrodite straight away. What with his particular liking for all things kissy kissy and all that!

Aphrodite was very beautiful indeed. She was more beautiful than Hera and Athena put together. Paris was very taken. Aphrodite walked around Paris as she spoke. Paris followed her with his eyes in the same way that a dog might look at a bone being walked about by its master.

"Paris," said Aphrodite, "you must ignore the promises made by Hera and Athena. You are not interested in their gifts. You know that. But I can give you something you want."

She asked him if he had heard of Helen of Sparta. Of course he had. Every single Human in the world had heard of her. She was said to be the most beautiful woman who had ever lived. Aphrodite said she would arrange for Helen to be his girlfriend if he chose Aphrodite to be the fairest of the three Goddesses. Paris couldn't believe what he was hearing.

"Really? You would do that for me? Do you mean it?" asked Paris, incredulously.

He asked her if he and Helen would be all lovey dovey kissy kissy if he chose her.

The Doctor turned to me and said that if this was an episode of Eastenders, the music would start up and the programme would finish and everybody would have to wait until next week to find out what happened next.

"Oh no! Don't even think about it! I couldn't bear the thought of having to wait a week to find out what happened next! It would drive me mad!" I said.

And besides, I hoped that it would not

be a week until we found the Time Machine and made our way back to our own time. But it was all right because we didn't have to wait very long to find out what happened next.

Paris did not even have to wait one minute before he made his mind up. I wonder if you have thought to which of the Goddesses you would have chosen to give the golden apple? No doubt, when you made up your mind, you thought about the consequences of what would happen when you made two of the Goddesses angry. You may already have guessed who Paris gave the apple to. Well, I think you are probably right. The thought of being all lovey dovey kissy kissy with the most beautiful woman in the world was too much for him. And so, without a moment's hesitation, Paris awarded the apple to Aphrodite.

Aphrodite was so pleased with herself that she had a broad grin all over her face. She tossed the apple up and down in her hand. It was as though the apple itself wasn't the really important thing. No, it seemed that the really important thing for Aphrodite was that she had won. She had beaten Hera and Athena. It was being chosen as the fairest that made her so happy.

Paris could hardly keep his feet on the ground at the thought of being all lovey dovey kissy kissy with Helen of Sparta, the most beautiful woman in all the world.

Helen's father was Zeus. Yes, old Zeus was her father as well! He had a lot of children, didn't he? Now, here is another storyline that you don't get on Eastenders:

Helen's mother didn't like Zeus because he was so old, and, anyway, she was happy the way she was. But Zeus knew that Helen's mother really liked swans, so he turned himself into a swan and she quite liked the look of him then.

Helen's beauty was talked about by just about everybody. Helen was already married, but Aphrodite promised Paris that she would definitely be his girlfriend. Paris was happier than any man alive. He could hardly keep still. He was skipping around like a spring lamb. You see, Helen was so beautiful that every young man would have liked her to be his girlfriend or wife, and quite a number of Gods wanted to marry her as well. In fact, Theseus, who slew the Minotaur, actually snatched Helen when she was still a child, but her brothers rescued her. Helen was so beautiful that her father's home was filled with young men as she approached marrying age. When eventually Helen did marry, it was her father's job to give gifts to the Gods. But he made a very serious mistake. He left one of the Gods out. That was a very serious mistake indeed because Gods like to take serious revenge if they are treated badly. The God who was left out decided that the revenge for this would be that Helen would leave her husband and go off with somebody else. Aphrodite knew this. Well, she would. She was the Goddess that had been left out. How very sneaky! Not only was she getting even with Helen's father for leaving her out, but she was also keeping her promise to Paris. Yes, Aphrodite was very clever indeed.

Paris became a Prince again before he met Helen. He was running a race in Troy when his real father recognised him and made him a Prince again. When Prince Paris visited Sparta, Helen fell in love with him instantaneously. They sneaked away together and were married and for some time they were very happy and they had three fine young sons. They lived in Troy and were much loved by all of the people of Troy. Helen was no longer known as Helen of Sparta - she was so loved by all the people of Troy that she became known as Helen of Troy.

I turned to Doctor Hoot and I told him that I loved a happy ending. Doctor Hoot said that he loved a happy ending as well. But there was a final twist that wasn't very happy at all. This story was not a comedy, it was a tragedy.

Helen's first husband was extremely angry at losing his wife. He gathered together the largest army that had ever been assembled and what happened next was something that you definitely would not get in Eastenders.

The Spartan army was so huge that it is believed that more people set off to conquer Troy than stayed at home. The battle that ensued was the most furious battle of all time. But the defence that Troy had was no match for the Spartan army. Troy was destroyed and nearly all of its people killed. Helen was brought back to her first husband in Sparta. Paris was put to death.

When Paris was about to be born, his mother had had a bad dream. Do you remember that she dreamt that when she looked down on her son, it was not a boy, but a burning log? And they went to consult a seer? Well, the seer turned out to be right because he said that, if the King did not kill his son, then all of their other children would die and Troy would be burned to the ground.

What a story that was! And you might wonder what happened to all of the Gods. Well, none of them died. But, you see, they couldn't, could they? They were immortal! The Greeks had lots of stories about Gods. You should try to find out more for yourself.

"I'd like you to take part in the play," said Sophocles, at the end of the story.

Pericles was a bit worried we might be offended that a God had been asked to take part in a play. But no, we looked quite keen and Pericles looked rather relieved that we weren't going to take it out on him.

Sophocles ushered us towards the back of the theatre and round the back where we could find costumes and some masks. Of course, in Ancient Greek theatres they all wore masks. Some of them looked really happy, some of them looked really sad, so you could tell people in the audience exactly how your character was feeling. The features were huge. The noses were big, even bigger than my nose. They had huge mouths so people right at the back could see as well. No women were allowed to act, so men had to play the parts of women!

I picked out a suitably scary mask and put it on. I found one for the Doctor

and he put it on as well. Then we stepped out onto the stage. By now the theatre was packed full of people, all staring down at us. I could see Pericles sitting there, looking around. He seemed to look quite worried. And then I worked out what it was. He was concerned at where I'd disappeared to. For the last two and a half days he had not let me out of his sight, but his Goddess Athena, as he thought, had all of a sudden disappeared. I could hear him, "Athena, Athena, where are you? Has anyone seen Athena?" What he didn't know was I was standing right in front of him, with a costume and mask on.

"Athena, where are you?"

All of a sudden, out of the corner of my eye, in the corner of the theatre, I noticed a very welcome sight. Can you guess what it was? Yes, it was the Time Machine. They'd hidden it in the theatre. The first place we'd wanted to go, and Pericles had hidden it where he thought we would never find it. The Doctor and I looked at each other, gave a quick thumbs up and the plan was in motion. We were going to try and sneak over to the Time Machine and get away in it before Pericles could stop us.

We sneaked over, stepped into the Time Machine – Pericles still hadn't noticed

147

- strapped ourselves in, quickly set the coordinates for home and pressed the start button. Of course, nothing happened. Oh no! I had forgotten, the Time Machine, of course, was still broken. How are we going to fix it?

Now, I don't know whether you know much about the mechanics of a Time Machine, but, well, to put it quite simply, the bit of the machine that had broken was a piece of string. Now, where were we going to find a piece of string in Ancient Greece? The Doctor looked up, pointing at my head.

"What? My head's not made of string," I said.

"No, no," he said. "The mask. It's held onto your head with a piece of string. Take off the mask, use the piece of string and we can get out of here and back in time for Eastenders."

"Brilliant!" I said. "But if I take my mask off, Pericles will see where I am hiding and he would definitely run over and try and stop us."

But it was our only chance. I quickly whipped off my mask and tied it onto the machine, but Pericles had already spotted us. He was heading over, waving his arms in the air.

"Athena, Athena, stop! Help! Athena is leaving."

I had just enough time to hit the start button on the Time Machine and the machine began to shake. The machine began to whirr, and the whole theatre began to fill with smoke.

As the smoke began to clear, we

were both more than relieved to see our surroundings. No more pillars and Greek statues. No more hot sunshine and no more sweaty feet wine. We were back right in the middle of my library in front of the roaring open fire that Mrs Broome had kept going for us for our return.

"Thank goodness for that," sighed the Doctor. "I had a great time but I really am glad to be back for one big reason."

"Don't tell me," I said. "Eastenders."

"Of course," said the Doctor, sloping off towards the television room. Ahh, what an adventure!

Thank you so much for reading my story. I do hope that you enjoyed it. I have definitely decided to have lots and lots more adventures. There is so much for me to find out about. I would love to find out a lot more about Greek Myths and Greek Theatre, so I think I shall have to go back and find out all about them. But there are so many other places and times to visit and find out about, such as the Romans and the Victorians. I don't know what I am more excited about. Visiting lots of different places or telling you all about them. I know that I am looking forward to doing both, so I had better get busy. I'll start planning a new trip just as soon as Doctor Hoot has finished watching Eastenders.

Amphora

The Greeks were very keen on making their own wine. Most houses had their own wine making room. Grapes were crushed, usually with the feet, and once ingredients were added to start the fermenting process, the wine was stored in huge Amphorae. From these, the wine could be poured into smaller amphorae as required. Each time it was poured, it was strained through a metal sieve to take out any imperfections (bits of toenails etc. Yummy!) This Amphora was probably used for decorative purposes and has a picture of the Goddess of Love, Aphrodite, on it.

Amphora

This Amphora was built for practical use and has even got a built in strainer in the neck. This would also keep flies out of the wine so, once it reached your party guests' mouths, the wine would be as clean as possible.

Arrow heads

These tiny arrow heads would have
originally been on the end of long sticks
with feathers on the far end. The shape
meant that, once shot into its intended
victim, it would be very hard to remove.
Some Ancient Greeks even loosened the
arrow heads before shooting to ensure
they would come off and be left inside
the victims body (nice!). The only way to
get these arrows out was to keep pushing
them in and pull them out of the back of
the poor victim!

Athena's Owl

Athena was always associated with an owl. This is where we get the phrase 'wise owl'. She was the Goddess of many things including Wisdom and the owl image even appears on a coin with her on the other side.

Coins

These are original 2500 year old Greek coins. The smallest ones are even smaller than our 5p!

Coins

These are copies of some of the best quality Ancient Greek coins that have been found. On these we can clearly see that the Ancient Greeks put pictures of their Gods and Goddesses onto their coins and not usually pictures of Kings and Queens. The one exception here is the coin on the left. This is a picture of Alexander the Great. The others carry pictures of Poseidon, Athena and Apollo.

Deltion

Paper was quite expensive in Ancient Greece so most schoolboys used a Deltion and wrote with a metal pen called a Stylus. A Deltion is a wooden board covered in wax and you could scratch letters into the wax or rub them out with the Stylus. To erase the whole board, the school teacher had a small fire that he could melt the wax with. The Romans were so impressed by this invention, they copied it and even made the first books by tying several Deltions together.

Discus

One event at the Olympic Games was the Discus. Competitors would have to throw this stone disc (about as big as your hand) as far as possible. This particular Discus has an inscription on it. The owner of this Discus was obviously so pleased to have won the event that he wrote his name on it and gave it as an offering at the Temple of Zeus. He dedicated it to two sons of Zeus, Castor and Pollux.

Epinetron

This weird object is my favourite "mystery object" but I can reveal to you now what it was used for. In Ancient Greece, the main material that their clothes were made from was wool. Wool's pretty hot stuff so they needed to make the threads as thin as possible so the final garments could be as light as possible. They would roll out the thread to the desired thickness on their knee and to protect their knee from getting sore, the Epinetron would fit over it. What a weird artefact?!

Greek Jug

This "Water Hydria", as the name suggests, was for carrying and pouring water. The Ancient Greeks had hundreds of different designs of pottery of every different function around the house.

Helmet

This helmet would have been worn by a soldier called a "Hoplite". An Ancient Greek's armour was quite minimal. They realised that if you cover yourself in heavy bronze then you can't move very quickly against an opponent. At the most, they would have a helmet, a breastplate and something called "Greaves". These were basically like football shin-pads but made of metal. A Hoplite would usually be armed with a sword, shield and spear.

Kylix

This piece of pottery is what most Ancient Greeks would drink from. This bowl could be shared by two people at a party. For bigger functions, they would bring out a bigger bowl/cup called a Krater. They could pass that around a whole room! Just imagine how much "sweaty feet wine" they must have drunk?!?!

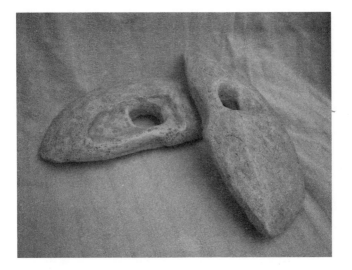

Long Jump Stones

Another event at the Olympic Games was the Long Jump. Whereas nowadays we do a bit of running before we jump, the Ancient Greeks did a jump from standing still! They would bend their knees and with a stone in each hand, they swung their arms backwards and then forwards, using the weight of the stones to carry them further. Cheating, I call it!?

Lyre

This was one of the Ancient Greeks' favourite instruments. Invented in Egypt, it was a sort of Harp/Guitar, usually with nine strings. They could pluck the Lyre and get quite a tune from it. Although it looks nice, take a look at the back of it to see what it's made of!

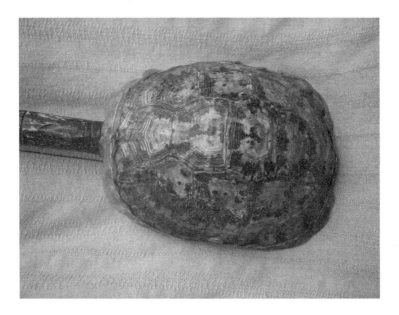

Lyre Reverse

Yes, it's made of a poor, dead tortoise's shell! Not only did a tortoise die for music, the Lyre is covered in goat's skin and the strings were sometimes made from the guts of dead cats! Nice, eh?

Mask

As you will know from my adventures in an Ancient Greek theatre, masks were an important part of theatre. The huge features on the masks let everyone know, even people on the back row, exactly what the character was like. The use of masks also meant that one person could play dozens of different characters.

Minoan Bull

The pottery workshops in Ancient Greece also made most of the toys. Any bits of clay left over from making pots could soon be turned into a toy animal like this or even dolls.

Oil Lamp

The only source of light in Ancient Greece was, of course, the oil lamp. The inside would be filled with olive oil and a small wick would be lit hanging out of the open end. Olive oil doesn't burn well and really needs to be hot in order to burn so the result was quite a smoky dull flame.

Papyrus

Another invention bought from the Ancient Egyptians was paper. They couldn't even use Papyrus in Egyptian schools. In Egypt the children had to write on broken bits of pottery! A few precious pieces of Papyrus would be looked after by the Ancient Greek teachers and used like we use text books today.

Shield

This leather covered shield would hopefully protect a soldier from the odd arrow or spear but it's quite heavy so it would probably have ended up getting in the way!

Shield detail

The centre of this shield has a finely carved mythical beast on it called a Gryphon. This maybe was hoped to scare enemies away but, if anything, it told other people which family you were from and which side you were on - a bit like football shirts today. The centre of the shield is called a Boss and it wouldn't only stop the odd blow from a sword. It could also be used to hit the enemy in the face. Ouch!

Spinning Top

Another toy from the pottery, these tops have been popular since they were invented and we still play with them today! You were supposed to wind the string around the top and set it spinning. Once spinning, you had to keep it going by whipping it with the string. Very tricky!

Sword detail

Weapons, like their shields, were always decorated with mythical animals or Gods. This sword includes snakes, lions and a rather rude man sticking his tongue out!

Sword detail

The top part of the sword, or Pommel, as it was called, is covered in a picture of an army marching to war and two ladies faces - possibly Gods protecting the owner of the sword or giving them strength.

Sword handle

The Ancient Greeks had quite short swords, like the Romans, and they were usually made of bronze. For a long time people have thought of bronze as too soft to make swords out of but recent tests have proved that iron swords could break and chip easily but bronze swords would last longer as they had more give in them.

Triple Oil Lamp

To try and make oil lamps more effective, someone made this triple one. With three flames it would, of course, make three times as much light. However, this 2500 year old lamp looks like it has been the cause of a huge fire in the past and it probably burned down the poor man's house!

# Other titles by E.R.Reilly

Harriet the Horrible

Best Friends

Rashnu

Tall Tales

Gnome Alone

One Boy, One Club, One Dream


Contact us at

SANTIAGO PRESS

PO BOX 8808

BIRMINGHAM

B30 2LR

santiago@reilly19.freeserve.co.uk


If you would like more information about Professor McGinty, then please visit his website at www.profmcginty.co.uk.